BEASTS OF OLYMPUS
GODS OF THE NORTH

LUCY COATS

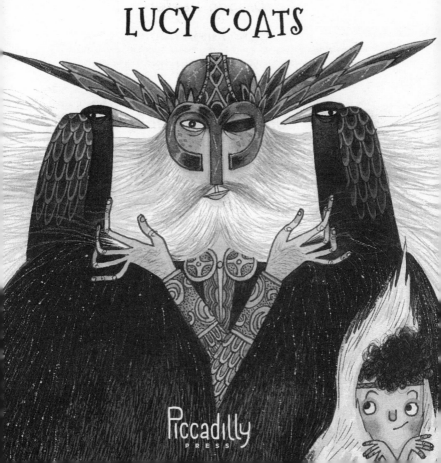

Piccadilly
PRESS

First published in Great Britain in 2018 by
Piccadilly Press
80–81 Wimpole Street, London, W1G 9RE
www.piccadillypress.co.uk

A CIP catalogue record for this book is available from the British Library.

ISBN: 978-1-848-12745-6

Typeset in opendyslexic
Printed and bound by Clays Ltd, Elcograf S.p.A.

Piccadilly Press is an imprint of Bonnier Zaffre,
a Bonnier Publishing Company
www.bonnierpublishingfiction.co.uk

For Al and Ray Preston,
with best wishes

1

Stranger!

Demon breathed out a secret sigh
of relief as he waved farewell to his
teacher. Chiron the centaur headed off
down the steep slope of Mount Pelion,
carrying a large bundle in his arms that
was cooing and gurgling. Baby Hygeia
was all cured now, so he was taking her
home to her parents at last. Demon
could finally get on with a full day of
quiet studying. Babysitting, he decided,
was a very tiring job. He much preferred
looking after his beasts. However,
Chiron liked him to write up his notes
on each case.

"That's so you can look up what you've done if it ever happens again," his teacher had said, when Demon had complained. "It's what all real healers do."

First of all, Demon put on his pink-tinted opticals and got out the beautiful red-and-gold-leather journal that the goddess Athena had given him after he had saved the phoenix from the terrible fire devils. He sucked the end of his quill for a moment and then began to form careful letters on the page as the pink light of dawn lit up the cave.

Babies: *How To Look After Them*, he wrote. But before he could get down another word, there was a whooshing sound outside the cave. A wisp of multicolored light snaked in and tapped him on the shoulder.

"That faun Bion is in trouble again," said Iris, goddess of the rainbow. "Hop in. You're needed back at the stables."

This time, Demon's sigh was loud and impatient. It was taking much longer than he'd expected to teach his brand-new assistant all the stuff he needed to know about the beasts in the Stables of the Gods. With Demon needing to explain everything about a hundred times, it was taking twice as long as it should have.

"What's he gone and done now?" Demon asked rather wearily as he climbed aboard the Iris Express. He wasn't sure he was cut out for being a teacher.

"I believe the griffin mentioned something about a bull fight and a pen on fire." Demon closed his eyes and clenched his jaw. This was the third incident in as many days. The two brass bulls were becoming a pain in his neck.

"You'd better hurry, Iris," he said.

"Hold onto your hair, then," said the rainbow goddess as she whisked him up and away to Olympus.

Demon pulled a neatly folded packet out of one of the rather messy drawers in the hospital shed and pointed to it with a stern finger.

"This," he said, waving it under the faun's nose, "is the Patent Pyro-

Protection Suit. Remember? The one you have to put on to keep yourself safe when the fiery beasts kick off. How many times have I told you that?"

Bion hung his head. Half the curly hair on his head was singed and smoking slightly, and one arm was red and burnt-looking.

"Sorry, Demon," he mumbled. "I forgot. Khalko and Kafto started fighting again, and then they got out and set the sun hay on fire, and I just panicked a bit. Some of it's all burnt and most of it's wet now. Doris was rather enthusiastic with the water buckets." Doris the Hydra was a helpful beast, but if it had been running with full buckets in all its nine mouths, Demon could just

5

imagine the sloshy mess it had made.

"Right," Demon said. "I'm fed up with those two bully boys. If they won't stop fighting and flaming, we'll have to separate them. Come on, you can help." He looked at Bion. "But first we'd better put some soothing ointment on those burns. I think I've got some left from when I treated the big winged horse."

Just as they were persuading a reluctant Khalko into entering his new fireproof pen, there was an unusual uproar outside.

"Hey, Pan's scrawny kid," said a familiar voice. "Come quick – something's happening!" It was Arnie the griffin, its orange eyes blazing with excitement. Demon latched the pen firmly, and then ran out with Bion.

Something was indeed happening. A chattering commotion came from a group of nymphs and cherubs hovering around a stranger who was clad in a long cloak of white furs and carrying a golden horn that twisted round his whole body like a giant snake. His hair was also white, and his white beard was plaited into three jutting forks. As Demon came closer, he saw that the man's eyes were the pale white-blue of an early winter sky.

"Who in the world is that?" he whispered to the griffin.

"Dunno," Arnie said. "Never seen him before."

The stranger put the horn to his lips and blew. It made a sound like no other Demon had ever heard, and suddenly his skin prickled as if he'd been dipped in deep, black water on the coldest-ever winter day. Then the stranger began to shout, and his voice filled the whole of Olympus.

"Hear me, hear me, O mighty Zeus. I am Heimdall, herald of Asgard, and I am sent to bring you news from the North." As he spoke, there was a crash of thunder, and Zeus appeared, with Hera beside him. As lightning flashed around them, and the sky darkened, the nymphs and cherubs all scattered and Demon shrank back behind a nearby olive tree. Arnie the griffin and Bion skulked in behind him.

"And what news is that, O herald of Asgard?" Zeus said, his voice booming just as loudly.

"Why, the best of news," said Heimdall, baring his golden teeth in a grin like a shark Demon had once seen down in Poseidon's realm. "The gods of the North are coming to visit you. It's party time! See ya later, Thunder Maker!" And then he disappeared in a blast of icy white light, leaving behind a large scroll fluttering through the air, and a huge pile of what looked like man-size stone jars.

"Well," said Hera, snatching the scroll and peering at it, before thrusting it at Zeus. "I call that very rude. Inviting themselves to stay like that. Who do these Northern gods think they are?"

She swept off, back to her palace, muttering, and Demon shrunk even further behind the tree, hoping she wouldn't see him. The Queen of the Gods wasn't exactly known for her sunny temper, and he didn't fancy being frazzled to a frizzle before he'd even seen what these new gods looked like.

Zeus frowned as he read the scroll, and as he stalked forward to examine the stone jars, a low mutter of thunder growled overhead. Picking one up as if it were a feather, he wrenched off the top with a pop and then looked inside, sniffing deeply as a cloud of foam spilled over the rim. Then he swung the jar up to his mouth and took a cautious swig of whatever was inside. All at once, a change came over his face. He took a great gulp, then another, and another.

"Ahhh," he sighed, wiping foam off his beard and setting the empty jar down and picking up another. "Mead! Delicious. Almost better than Dionysus's grape brew." Straightening up to his full height, his eyes swept round Olympus, finally settling on Demon, who automatically began to quake with fear. But whatever Zeus had drunk seemed to have put him in a good mood.

"Ah, Pandemonius," he said. "I want every last inhabitant of Olympus outside my palace before Helios and his chariot have reached the midpoint of the sky. Run round and tell them all, would you?"

"Y-Yes, Your Mighty Thunderousness," Demon said, dropping to his knees. Then a thought hit him. "Er, do you mean I'm to tell the other gods and goddesses, too?" he asked cautiously.

Zeus laughed. "Hera will have let most of them know already, but you'd better pop up to Hephaestus's forge. He never hears anything if he's banging about with those great hammers of his. Hurry up now, young Stablemaster. There's no time to lose." With that he picked up yet another of the enormous stone jars and set off after Hera, humming a tune that sounded like stars grinding against each other.

Demon looked up at the sky. Helios's chariot didn't have much further to go before the sun would be right overhead. Panic started to sink in when the griffin poked him in the back with its sharp beak.

"I'll let the nymphs and dryads know, Pan's scrawny kid," it said. "And they'll tell the cherubs."

"And I'll tell the other fauns from the kitchen," said Bion, rather squeakily. An encounter with Zeus tended to make almost anyone a bit squeaky, Demon had found.

Thanking them over his shoulder, Demon ran as fast as he could up the mountain to find his old friend the blacksmith god, Hephaestus. Taking a quick look to make sure the dragon-mode danger sign wasn't anywhere in sight, he leapt over the Colchian Dragon's purple tail and ran into the dark, sooty cave. He followed the ringing sound of hammer on anvil to its source. Hephaestus had a grimy rag wrapped around his sweaty forehead, and he was battering away at a long sword that glowed cherry red from the heat of the fire. Demon jumped up and down to get the smith god's attention, and with one last mighty blow, Hephaestus plunged the sword into a nearby water trough, causing an explosion of hissing and steam.

"What?" he said, scowling. "I'm busy. Ares needs this sword by tonight. He's got another wretched war to fight."

"Never mind that," said Demon, panting and wheezing. "Zeus wants everyone outside the palace right now. He sent me to fetch you."

Muttering, the smith god put down his hammer. "Don't eat all the charcoal while I'm gone, Colin," he said to the dragon. But it took no notice, snoring quietly in the corner on a pile of golden armlets.

"Now, what's going on, young Pandemonius?" he asked. "And since when have you been my father's messenger?"

Panting even harder and running to keep up with the god's long strides, Demon explained. And as they got nearer to Zeus and Hera's palace, the sound of a great crowd rose to greet them.

"Scoot over, Pan's scrawny kid," said Arnie the griffin, joining them as Demon and Hephaestus squeezed past a chattering gaggle of fauns, Bion among them. "I'm not missing this."

And then, with a golden flash,
Zeus was on the balcony above them
with Hera and all the other gods and
goddesses crowded in behind him. He
held up a hand, and immediately there
was silence.

"Odin and the Gods of Asgard arrive
in seven days," he said. "I want every
flower polished, every palace painted.
Olympus must be perfect. We will
not be shamed before the gods of the
North, will we?"

"NO!" came the reply, so that
Olympus shook with the force of it.

2

Wings on Fire

"You've got some tidying up to do,
Pan's scrawny kid," said Arnie, reaching
out a claw and patting some mucky
straw blowing about.

Demon looked around. It was true.
The Stables weren't as immaculate
as he would have liked. There were
cobwebs in some of the corners, and
Doris the Hydra had dropped a messy
trail of ambrosia crumbs on the floor.
He sniffed. There was also a distinct
smell of burnt hay, mixed with a bit
of a pooey stench.

"Come on, Bion," he said. "Let's find the buckets." But Bion was staring at something over Demon's shoulder. All at once, the faun gasped and fell flat on his face.

Demon whipped round.

Zeus was standing right there, leaning against the huge doorframe, with Eagle perched on one shoulder. Demon's knees began to tremble. This was definitely not the happy Zeus of earlier that day. He was rubbing his temples as if he had a headache.

The King of the Gods scowled, and Demon braced himself. Was this it? Was Zeus going to zap him into charcoal at last? He squeezed his eyes shut and hunched his shoulders tight round his ears, waiting.

"PANDEMONIUS!" The great, booming voice rang out, making Demon's eyes pop open despite his fear. His mouth was dry as an empty well, but he forced himself to speak.

"Y-yes, Your Tremendous Thunderousness. H-how can I help you?"

Zeus bent down and picked Demon up with one thumb and finger, so that he was dangling just in front of Zeus's nose.

"Listen well, young Stablemaster! You will perform with some of your flying horses as part of the entertainment after the feast. Make it magnificent, make it memorable. I leave it to you, boy."

He cast a piercing blue eye over the Stables, wrinkling his nose. "Get rid of the smell, too. I want this place and every beast in it polished to perfection. I shall be giving our guests the grand tour of Olympus."

Demon didn't dare move, terrified that Zeus was going to drop him. The god glared at him.

"DO I MAKE MYSELF CLEAR?" he barked. Demon found himself nodding so hard he thought his head was going to drop off.

"Yes, Your Superb Scariness," he whispered. "I understand."

Without quite knowing how, he found himself on the ground again, all in a

heap. Zeus was nowhere to be seen,
Bion was sobbing in a corner, and even
the griffin had its wings over its eyes.

Demon's mind was racing. An aerial
display with the winged horses. He
could do that, and maybe he could get
the boss horse Keith to . . . His mind
ground to a halt suddenly, remembering,
and his stomach dropped like a stone.

Of course!

All the winged horses were down on
earth. Iris had refused to carry them
ever again after they pooed all over
her. He had no way of getting them
back up to Olympus.

"Oh no," he groaned. "What am I
going to do?"

"Do about what?" asked the griffin.

Demon explained.

"Sounds like you're in trouble again, Pan's scrawny kid," Arnie said, yawning. "I'm off for a nap. Gods make my beak ache. And if you think you're roping me in to this aerial performance thingy, then think again." With that, it stalked off and lay down in its pen, all four paws in the air.

"I've got an idea," said Bion, timidly. "If Iris won't do it, what about Golden Dog? Couldn't he bring the horses back?"

Demon nearly hugged him. Golden Dog had the strange ability of slipping through the cracks in time and space,

and he could take people along with
him.

"Brilliant!" he said. "Well done, Bion.
Let's go and find him right now."

Bion blushed with pleasure.

Unfortunately, Golden Dog was not in
his usual place, curled up with the magic
nanny goat, Amaltheia.

"Mehhh!" she bleated as he entered
her luxurious pen. "Was that my little
Zeusie I heard shouting? Why didn't he
come and see me?"

"I think he was a bit busy," Demon
said. "I'm sure he'll be in to see you
soon. Now, do you know where Golden
is?"

"He left this morning," Amaltheia said. "I don't know where he went. He never tells me anything, silly hound."

"Can you call him back?" Demon pleaded. "It's really urgent."

The old goat butted him in the leg.

"I'll try," she said. "As it's you, young Pandemonius. But mind you get one of those nice nymphs to come and comb out my curls for me."

She closed her eyes and let out three high, clear bleats, then three very low ones. Almost at once, there was a distant bark, sounding as if it were coming from the end of a very long tunnel, and then, in a frantic flurry of legs, waving tail, and tiny golden stars, the dog appeared out of nowhere.

Once the usual ritual of bouncing and jumping up and snuffly licking of faces was done, Demon explained what he needed.

"Ooh! Fun!" Golden Dog barked. "Grab my ears, then, Demon! Let's go!"

Demon had done this before, but the dizzy, whooshing sensation still made his stomach feel as if it were falling out of his feet. Within less than a breath, though, he was stumbling onto the sunny slope where the winged horses liked to graze. As he and Golden Dog appeared out of nowhere, the herd whinnied in alarm and took off into the air.

"It's all right," Demon called to them. "It's only me!" Slowly the little horses settled to earth again, and Keith, the boss horse, trotted up to him, his daughter Sky Pearl behind him.

"Oh!" said Demon. "When did you get back?" He'd left Sky Pearl with his friend Prince Peleus in the Mountains of Burning Sand after their adventure with the phoenix.

"Today-hey-hey," she whinnied. "I dropped Peleus off at his dad's palace. They gave me minty sweeties." She nuzzled his tunic. "I LIKE minty sweeties!"

"I'll make you some," Demon promised. "But now you all have to come back to Olympus with Golden Dog and me. Zeus needs us. Get into a line and hold on to each other's tails!"

He turned to Golden Dog, keeping his fingers crossed that the idea would work.

"We'd better do this in twos and threes."

By the time all the little horses had finally staggered into their paddock, looking a bit stunned by the short journey, Helios had nearly driven his sun chariot over the horizon. Demon and Bion brought them a big barrowful of unburnt sun hay.

"You can rest tonight," he said. "But first thing tomorrow, we have a performance to plan!"

Demon lay awake under his spider-silk blanket. He and Bion had started in on scrubbing every inch of the Stables before they went to bed. His body was exhausted, but his mind refused to shut down. Magnificent and memorable was what Zeus had demanded. But how was he going to make sure his aerial display was both?

"Maybe gold paint," he muttered. "Or streamers . . ."

"Whaa . . .?" murmured Bion sleepily from the next-door pallet.

"Never mind," Demon whispered. Eventually, he dozed off, but his dreams were full of wings and fire.

The next morning, Demon set Bion to
boiling up a small pot of peppermint
leaves and honey for Sky Pearl's
sweeties, and a much bigger pot of
eucalyptus leaves, lemons and pine
needles.

"We have to make the poo chute
smell nice," he said. "This should do it."
He wasn't sure that the hundred-armed
monsters at the bottom of the poo
chute were going to appreciate the
nice smell much, but they'd just have
to put up with it.

When Demon arrived at the paddock,
the winged horses were in an excited
huddle of wings and hooves.

"Look De-he-he-mon!" Keith whinnied.
Whirling round, he and Sky Pearl set off

at a canter, one swerving left and the other right, with half the herd following each of them. They soared into the air and began a complicated series of loop-the-loops and spirals high in the sky. Then they came together behind Keith in a big V and swooped down low over Demon's head, so that he was nearly knocked over by the breeze of their wings.

He clapped his hands.

"Amazing!" he yelled. But it was still not quite marvellous or memorable enough. How could he make the display good enough so that Zeus wouldn't spike him with a lightning bolt? Suddenly he remembered his dreams of the night before. Wings . . . and fire.

"Keep practising!" he called. "I've got an idea." And he started to run up the mountain towards Hephaestus's forge.

When he got there, the forge was buzzing with activity. Golden automatons were running about everywhere, and the place was full of heat and sparkle. Piles of purple and orange fire-jewels lay everywhere, along with rubies and pearls and all manner of other gemstones. Hephaestus hunched over a delicate piece of jewellery, alternately teasing out strands of gold with a tiny pair of tongs and tapping them with a small silver hammer.

"Can I borrow Colin, please?" Demon shouted, waving a hand towards the enormous purple dragon curled up on the charcoal heap.

"Take him with pleasure!" Hephaestus said, not looking up. "We're all tripping over him. You'd be doing me a favour. I've got to make enough jewellery for all the goddesses, as well as gifts for all our visitors." He wiped a sweaty hand over his forehead and started tapping again.

"What do you need me for?" asked the Colchian Dragon, snatching up a last mouthful of charcoal. His bright purple tail made a slithery sound on the rocks.

"You'll see," said Demon. He crossed his fingers as he spoke, though, because there was a big danger that it could all go horribly wrong.

3

The Ship of Clouds

"Like this, but a lot bigger." Demon sketched a large circle in the air with his hand. "Do you think you can do it?"

Colin the Colchian Dragon blinked lazily and let out a tiny charcoally belch.

"What happens if I get scared and, you know . . ." the dragon nodded towards its back end. When Demon had first met Colin, the dragon had been the fartiest creature ever, and had nearly blown Olympus to smithereens.

"You won't," said Demon firmly. "And anyway, I thought the charcoal-and-peppermint diet fixed all that."

"Oh, well," said the dragon. "I'll give it a go." It drew in a deep breath and turned its muzzle to the sky. Then, very gently, it puffed out. With a little *pop*, a perfect ring of fire floated into the air, widening as it went, then another and another.

Demon punched a fist into the air. "YES!" He turned to the little pegasus. "Now, Keith, let's see if you and the herd can fly through the rings."

A few days (and a couple of nearly singed wingtips) later, Colin the dragon and Keith's team of winged horses had

put together a display that even Demon
thought was magnificent and marvellous
enough for the gods. He'd persuaded
one of the nymphs to make some
flower-petal-and-silver-ribbon streamers
for him, and he and Bion were going to
braid them into all the horses' manes
and tails just before the performance.
Zeus had sent over the running order
– the winged horses were to close the
show, and he'd also sent over strict
instructions as to what they were to
do at the very end. Demon just hoped
it would work.

Meanwhile, all the beasts in the
stables had been shampooed and
polished and brushed till they shone,
though the giant scorpion had objected
rather violently and tried to sting Doris
the Hydra to death. Not a speck of dust

or dirt remained. Every instrument in the hospital shed gleamed, and every bandage was snowy white. Even the poo chute sparkled, though the hundred-armed monsters were not at all happy with their new poo-plus-eucalyptus drain cleanser diet.

Demon looked round.

"I think we're ready," he said to Bion and the griffin. As he spoke, a large fluffy white cloud sailed across the sky.

"Oh no," said Bion. "I hope it isn't going to rain."

"That's no rain cloud, Faun Boy," said Arnie. "Look!" The griffin pointed with a claw.

Demon's mouth fell open in a silent O of wonder, and he began to run. It seemed that all the other inhabitants of Olympus had the same idea, and soon a large chattering crowd had gathered.

Under the cloud, a huge sailing ship was gliding down towards Olympus, long and sleek, with round shields lining its sides. In a series of rainbow flashes all the Olympian gods appeared, just as the ship slid gracefully to a halt.

It brought with it an icy breeze filled with the scent of cold, wild places – and also a slight smell of goat. A golden gangplank slid out of the ship's side, and a tall, fierce-looking god strode down it, his long hair and beard floating like tangled white thistledown about his face. He wore a magnificent silver-winged helmet and had a leather patch over his left eye. On each of his shoulders perched an enormous black raven.

Beside the fierce god was an equally tall, snow-pale goddess wearing a crown of diamond icicles. Behind them came a huge golden-haired god carrying a gigantic silver hammer, and then nine other gods and goddesses, including a tall, shifty-eyed figure right at the back, with a pointy beard and a silver helmet with a shiny green gem stuck to it.

Demon couldn't see the god at the back very well. The figure seemed to slip in and out of view, blurring and changing shape, so that suddenly he was a proud mare, a leaping salmon, and then a tiny bright green fly that buzzed off out of sight.

As soon as they had disembarked, the raven god turned to the cloud ship and clicked his fingers. All at once, the ship began to fold itself up, smaller and smaller until it lay at his feet, no bigger than a handkerchief. Demon's mouth dropped open as the god picked it up and put it in a pocket, but there was no time to wonder.

As Zeus and Hera stepped forward to greet the gods of the North, Apollo struck a chord on his silver lyre, and roses rained down out of the sky, making a sweet-smelling path before them.

"Greetings, Odin and all you gods of Asgard," Zeus boomed, and out of nowhere he produced a huge golden cup brimming with Dionysus's special red party drink. "Let us drink to friendship and harmony, then let us feast."

From among the crowd of nymphs, fauns, cherubs and other beings, Demon watched anxiously. What if the Asgardians didn't like Dionysus's brew? What if they spat it out and then there was a war between the gods? The whole world might be frazzled to a frizzle. But all scary thoughts went right out of his head when Odin took the cup and drained it in one gulp.

"Good stuff," he said, clapping Zeus familiarly on the back. "Now, where's that feast you mentioned, Thunder Maker. I'm starving, and this wretched ceremonial helmet is far too hot."

Odin made an impatient gesture at his head, and suddenly the winged helmet was no longer there. In its place was a rather disreputable wide-brimmed hat, tilted over Odin's eye-patch to shade his face from the bright Olympian light.

It was the most magnificent spread Demon had ever seen, with laden tables stretched all around the beautiful garden that lay outside the palaces of the gods. Hestia and her kitchen helpers had outdone themselves, especially in the dessert department. Demon, however, was too nervous about the forthcoming performance to do more than nibble on a couple of his favourite honey cakes.

The gods were seated at the high table, a wondrous creation of snowy marble inlaid with ebony and gold olive branches. Every god and goddess had a different chair, each adorned with living symbols. Hera's was covered in blinking peacock-feather eyes and Zeus's sizzled with tiny lightning bolts. Demon noticed that Odin's was covered with soaring ravens, but the two birds that had arrived with him were nowhere to be seen. He wondered for a moment where they'd gone, but just then the toasts started. It was nearly time.

"Come on, Bion," Demon whispered.

They both crept away from the feast and ran to the Stables. Keith, Sky Pearl and the rest of the fliers were in a high state of excitement as the sparkling flower streamers were attached.

"You look magnificent," said Demon.
"Now, where's that dragon? Is he in
position?" Running outside, he checked
high up on the mountainside. Yes, there
was a splash of purple above, and
higher still in the blue sky, two black
dots circled.

Demon frowned. Were those Odin's
ravens? He hoped they wouldn't get in
the way.

"Come on," he said. "Time to go. Wait
for Zeus's sky signal – and remember,
no pooing on anyone's head!"

His heart beating faster than a
running deer's, Demon went back to
the feast. Catching Zeus's eye, Demon
nodded. The horses were ready.

"We have a little surprise to welcome you, our honoured godly guests," Zeus boomed. "So sit back and enjoy the show."

With that, Hermes lifted a golden trumpet to his lips and blew one high note. First the nymphs danced, then the dryads performed a ballet with their trees, which twined about them like living partners. Hades had brought his skeleton guard with him, and they had a mock battle with some of Ares's soldiers, which ended with rather too many severed bony limbs for Demon's liking.

Hades had also brought Demon's friend Orpheus with him. The misty musician played his ghostly lyre so beautifully that it made everyone weep.

Flocks of kingfishers zipped through the air like tiny blue jewels.

The audience's tears were soon turned to laughter when the cherubs and fauns did a funny little skit, imitating all the Olympians. Demon didn't know how they dared. Then Zeus held up his hand for silence.

"And now for our grand finale," he said. With that, he took a lightning bolt from his eagle, twirled it, and flung it upwards, where it burst, turning the sky to incandescent whiteness.

The little winged horses took to the air in pairs, forming a huge circle above the feasting gods. Then they went into their routine. They flew so fast that the streamers looked like darting rainbows,

weaving patterns of loops and curls
that looked like intricate writing across
the white sky.

When the dragon's fire hoops
appeared in the air, the gods and
goddesses whooped and cheered as
the horses flew through and in and out
of them. The final hoop floated down
towards the feast, getting bigger and
bigger, straightening out into a rope of
fire. Demon crossed his fingers and toes
and everything else crossable. If this
last bit didn't work . . .

The horses formed into pairs again,
and with one last loop-the-loop, Sky
Pearl and Keith arrowed low towards
the very ends of the fire rope, which
they grabbed in their mouths. Flying
even lower over the high table, they

dropped the fire rope right over the
gods and goddesses, where it burst
in a shower of popping golden stars.
And when the stars had cleared,
each goddess was wearing a fabulous
bracelet of sparkling jewels, and each
god a spectacular armband.

"Magnificent!" shouted Odin, banging
on the table with one enormous fist
as the horses soared away back to the
Stables. "The best yet!" And all the
other Asgardians and Olympians agreed.

After receiving a congratulatory clap
on the back from his dad, Pan, and an
approving nod from Zeus, Demon nipped
up to Hephaestus's forge to thank
Colin the Colchian Dragon for his help.
He then went back to the Stables to
make sure Keith and his herd had extra

ambrosia and hay, and to give them big pats. Later, after one last inspection of the stables, he crept into bed and, snuggling down under his spider-silk blanket, closed his tired eyes and listened to the sound of Bion's little whiffling snores.

As he slid into sleep, a shiny black feather drifted down from the rafters above, and two shadows swooped down over him. But Demon was too tired to notice.

4

An Unexpected Journey

"Incoming," hissed Arnie the griffin, peering outside. "Incoming gods."

Demon and Bion had been up since before Eos threw back her pink dawn curtains, giving everything and everyone in the Stables a final polish.

"Right, everyone," Demon said to the beasts. "Best behaviour, all of you. And, Doris, remember not to drool on the visitors." With that, he and Bion ran to the doors and flung them wide open, standing to attention with Arnie between them. The griffin had somehow persuaded Hephaestus to make it a golden collar and claw shields, and was wearing them proudly.

Zeus was striding towards them, with Odin beside him, ravens on his shoulders, and two other Asgardians trailing behind.

"Blimey, Pan's scrawny kid," said Arnie, out of the side of its beak. "It's the two big chiefs and the pretty ones. Better watch your manners."

Demon was watching his manners so hard that his knees wobbled. He didn't even slap at the annoying bright green fly that was buzzing around his ear, for fear of being misunderstood.

"Well, Stablemaster?" said the King

of the Gods. "Are you ready for us?"

"Yes, Your Thundery Tremendousness, we are," he said, bowing low. The griffin beside him tried to execute a sort of curtsey but got tangled in its own legs and fell over. Embarrassed, Arnie sat down and began to preen its wing feathers.

"Sorry about that, Your Marvellousnesses," Demon said, blushing. It was not a good start. "Come right this way." But then he stopped. Odin was holding up a hand. Tiny snowflakes fell from his fingers, melting as they hit the ground.

"Just one moment, Thunder Maker." Suddenly his one green eye seemed to pierce Demon's skin, sucking out all his secrets, and then his ravens took off, gliding towards Demon on silent wings. As they swooped down, they plucked a single hair from each side of his head, then soared off back to their master. Landing on his shoulders again, they cawed quietly into his ears. Demon let out a muffled "ouch" and began to shake like a leaf in a high wind. Had he done something wrong? Was this the beginning of being slowly torn to death by raven pecks? But then Zeus was speaking.

"Is something the matter with my Stablemaster, One-Eye?" he said, a slight edge to his voice.

Odin slung an arm over Zeus's shoulder. "Not a thing, old boy," he said. "In fact, he's the reason we're really here. We need to borrow him."

If Demon's mouth had fallen open any further, it would have hit his toes.

"M-m-me, Your Serene Snowiness?" he stammered. "But why?"

"Yes, why do you need MY Stablemaster," said Zeus, his bushy eyebrows giving off little sparks of lightning. "Don't you have one of your own?"

"Well, we've got a little problem we hope he can fix," Odin said. "But I'll let the twins explain."

A god and a goddess stepped forward. They were both so incredibly golden that Demon could hardly look at them without being dazzled.

"I am Freya. What is your name, young Stablemaster?" the goddess asked. She wore a cloak of shining bronze falcon feathers, and her voice was soft as a summer breeze.

"P-Pandemonius, Your Gorgeous Goldenosity," he stuttered.

Freya smiled, and her teeth were white as pearls. Demon tried hard not to fall over.

"Oh, I LIKE him, Frey!" she said to her brother. "None of you ever call me nice names."

"Never mind that," said the equally beautiful god. "Pandemonius, is it true that you've had some success in healing incurable immortal beasts?"

Demon blushed. "Well, I s-suppose so," he said modestly. "Kind of. I, er . . . I haven't had many failures so far."

"Are you good with pigs?"

"Um," Demon said slowly. "I haven't dealt with one of those yet."

"Here's the thing," said Frey. "My old boar, Goldbristle, is losing his light. I drive along in the sky, and he just gets dimmer and dimmer."

"He's simply not shining properly any more," said Freya. "Everything's all dark and horrid now in Asgard. And that means the plants are dying. None of the new crops I've planted have grown at all, and poor Idunn's apple trees are positively drooping."

"The long and short of it," Odin interrupted, "is that your friend Pegasus was talking to my horse, Sleipnir, and telling him how you'd helped heal his wounds. So I sent my ravens, Thought and Memory, to check up on you, and it seems you've got quite the reputation among the creatures of the world. The phoenix was particularly complimentary, they tell me. So there it is. Will you come back to Asgard with us and see if you can find out what's wrong with our boar Goldbristle? None of our healers have a clue what's up with the old chap."

He cleared his throat and turned to Zeus. "That's if you don't mind, of course, Thunder Maker," he said, narrowing that one green eye.

Zeus stroked his beard thoughtfully. "That depends," he said, "on the state in which we find these Stables, and the beasts within. I wouldn't want to lend you a Stablemaster whose charges weren't up to scratch."

With that, he strode past Demon, whose heart had just somersaulted into his throat and was doing a little fear dance on his tonsils. What if things weren't up to scratch enough?

Demon shuddered, and followed the four gods in, trailed by a nervous-looking Bion. *I might as well know the worst right away*, he thought, as the griffin disappeared out of sight. He didn't blame it.

Zeus and his companions poked

into everything. Luckily, all the beasts behaved, and the little winged horses were given special ear scratches and praise, though Amaltheia did try to scold Zeus for not visiting her.

Before the King of the Gods could do more than twitch an eyebrow, Demon managed to shut the goat up with a handful of Sky Pearl's peppermint sweeties, which stuck her jaws together.

"What are those scars?" Freya asked, pointing to the Hydra's nine necks.

The old anger rose up in Demon's chest, driving out any fear. "Poor Doris," he said, stroking the green head that was lovingly draped over his shoulder. "Horrible Heracles chopped all the Hydra's heads off, so I had to stick them

back on. I couldn't get rid of the scars,
though."

Demon kept his fingers crossed,
praying that none of the gods would ask
how he'd done it. He still wasn't sure
that using one of Hera's magic golden
apples had been entirely legal – and
there was the worry that the tiny drip
of juice that he had licked off his finger
had made him a bit more immortal than
he should be. Nobody but Offy and
Yukus, his magical healing snakes, knew
about that – and Demon wanted to keep
it that way.

"Impressive," said Odin, and Demon
glowed. He didn't often get praise from
a god.

Then Zeus made him show them

everything in the hospital shed.

"What's that?" Frey asked, pointing to the silver box that stood, shiny and polished, in the centre of his operating table.

"This is the magic medicine box Hephaestus made me, Your Gloriousness. Say hello, box," Demon said, tapping it.

The magic medicine box let out a sudden stream of sparks and started to glow blue, making Frey jump a little.

"Exiting standby mode," it said. "Please wait." A tiny rainbow circle began to spin in its lid, then went out.

"State nature of medical problem," it said in its usual tinny voice.

Demon sighed.

"Just greet the gods nicely, please," he said, trying not to sound cross.

The box emitted a rude raspberry sound. Demon went bright red.

"I'm so sorry, Your Magnificent Majesties," he said. "I think it might have picked up another bug. I'll take it back to Hephaestus." Grabbing a linen cloth, he threw it over the box, hiding it. He knew perfectly well it didn't have a bug really. It was just being its usual grumpy self.

"We've seen enough," said Zeus. "If you can promise me that your assistant is capable of handling things in your absence, Pandemonius, then I think you may go to Asgard. I am very pleased with you indeed."

"Th-thank you, Your Tremendous Thunderiness," he said, dropping to his knees as Zeus stretched down a hand to pat the top of his curly head.

"I think I'd better give you the gift of the tongues of men and gods," he said. "Not everyone in Asgard will speak our language as well as Odin and the rest of our visitors."

A sharp tingle ran through Demon's scalp, and his brain suddenly felt as if it had stretched to twice its size. He reached up a hand to check, but his head seemed to be the normal shape it always had been.

Zeus turned to Odin.

"I'd better send Demeter with you, too," he said. "My sister is good at crops and all that. And she's always a bit down when Persephone's with Hades. A trip to Asgard will cheer her up."

"It's settled, then," said Odin. "Now let's go and find some more of Dionysus's brew. I must persuade him to tell me how he makes it." He looked at Demon. "Go and pack, young Pandemonius. We leave at dawn."

The next morning the cloud ship was ready, rocking in the small breeze. Demon clutched a bag of the warmest clothes he could lay his hands on, plus the magic medicine box, his dad's pipes, and all the supplies he thought he might need. He'd even borrowed a bit of Hestia's fire, just in case. She'd given it to him with the usual warnings not to let Zeus know he had it, so it was stowed at the very bottom of his bag.

"I hear it's cold up there," said Melanie the nymph, as he was saying his goodbyes to everyone. "You might need a cloak."

"Bring me back a nice bit of meat," said Arnie the griffin, giving him a sharp peck of farewell.

"Don't worry," said Bion. "I'll take care of everyone." Demon just hoped that was true. Bion wasn't the most reliable of helpers. But there was nothing he could do about it.

As the Asgardians came down from Zeus and Hera's palace, Demon felt a tap on his shoulder. He turned round to see his dad standing there, looking uncharacteristically worried.

"You take care up there, my boy," Pan said, bending down to give him a god hug that smelled, as usual, of pungent green things, blood and old goaty musk.

"I will, Your Dadness," he said.

But Pan hadn't finished. "Your mum had a dream about you a few nights ago. She made me swear to warn you not to go anywhere near any dark ice caves. Apparently she saw you in one – and you were in danger. I won't be able to help you in the North. It's too far for the pipes to reach if you're in trouble."

"I'll take care," Demon promised. "I've got my phoenix feather and some sandalwood with me, in case of dire emergencies. Look!" He peeled back the shoulder of his tunic to show the precious things bound against his chest with a linen bandage.

"That's good," said his dad. "Glad to see you're prepared for anything, my boy."

As Demon walked away, a shiver trailed a cold finger down his spine. He didn't fancy the idea of a dangerous dark ice cave one little bit.

Just as he was about to go aboard, Zeus beckoned Demon over.

"Behave yourself, and don't let me down, Stablemaster," he said. "Or I may just give you to Eagle for a snack." Eagle was on his shoulder and clacked its beak menacingly, right by Demon's ear.

Demon walked onto the ship, feeling a bit lost. He stood at the stern, looking back as Olympus faded into the distance, wondering how long he'd be gone for, and if Bion would really manage on his own. There was no turning back now, though. He was on his own.

5

Thrud

Demon soon left the stern and went forward to stand at the prow, which was shaped like the jaws of a ravening wolf. He'd only been there for a short while, marvelling at the cloudscapes that spread out before him, when the deck started to shake and he heard the unmistakable sound of godly footsteps behind him.

Whirling round, Demon saw the god with the huge hammer approaching. What should he do? Should he bow? Should he fall to his knees? He didn't know how to act around these new deities at all. In the end, he compromised, going to one knee and bowing his head.

"Hey!" said the god, in a voice like the clang of swords. "None of that, young Pandemonius. Get up and face me like a man!"

Demon scrambled to his feet. "S-sorry, Your Humungous Hammeriness," he said.

"We don't go in for all that bowing and scraping in the North," the god continued, sticking out a massive iron-gloved hand towards Demon. "I'm Thor, by the way. Champion of Asgard."

Demon stuck out his own hand, rather

timidly. As Thor took it and shook it, though, Demon shot up high into the air and was only just caught by the cloud sails.

"By Odin's eye!" said Thor from the deck below, unhooking his hammer. "I forget my own strength sometimes. Fetch, Mjölnir!"

With that Thor flung his hammer right at Demon. Before he'd even had time to duck, the hammer had curled around Demon's body like a huge hand and flown him back down to the deck at Thor's feet.

"Hmm," said Thor, looking at him. "I think I'd better get my daughter, Thrud, to sort you out when we get to Asgard. She's more your size."

The first thing that Demon noticed was
that Asgard was FREEZING! As Frey
had warned, it was also very dark and
gloomy, though Demon had somehow
half expected the sunlight that shone
on Olympus to shine on Asgard too.
There was a deep coat of white stuff
on the ground and big, fat ice spears
dangled from everything.

Although he'd already put on all the
clothes he'd brought, Demon began to
shiver almost immediately, and his bare
toes started to turn blue. The only
spot of warmth he had was the phoenix
feather bound to his chest, which
seemed to be sending out a small pulse
of heat that he was very thankful for.

All the gods and goddesses pushed

past him and hurried off the cloud ship
as soon as it landed, so Demon was
left lost and not knowing where to go.
Dragging his belongings towards the
nearest building, he stumbled along,
hugging himself and wishing he'd never
heard of Asgard. How was he supposed
to cure Goldbristle if he didn't even
know where the poor beast was to be
found?

Then it got worse. More of the white
stuff started to fall, thick fluffy flakes
of it covering his head and shoulders
in seconds. Demon could see nothing.
Suddenly, he heard a shout just by his
left ear.

"Hey! Are you Pandemonius?"

"Y-y-yes," he tried to say, but his

teeth were chattering so hard he could hardly get the word out. A hand grabbed his arm and yanked him through a door into a large room full of firelight. The wooden walls gave off the fragrant scent of pine, which mixed with the delicious smells coming from a large cauldron on the fire.

Demon blinked the white stuff out of his eyes and saw a girl standing in front of him. She had hair the colour of ripe corn, tied into a multitude of braids, and she wore a long cloak of blue heron feathers lined with fluffy down, over a thick woollen tunic and breeches.

"Hello," she said. "I'm Thrud Thorsdaughter. My dad sent me to take care of you." She looked Demon up and down, her eyes widening at his thin layers and open-toed sandals, as he gazed enviously at her cosy-looking boots. "Are those really all the clothes you wear in Olympus?" she asked.

Demon nodded. "I-it's a lot w-warmer there," he said, through his chattering teeth. "And p-please c-call me D-Demon."

Thrud rummaged in a chest and pulled out a blanket. "Wrap this around you and help yourself to soup, Demon," she said, pointing to the cauldron. Then, with a flash of blue feathers, she was gone.

By the time Demon had eaten three bowls of soup and unfrozen his toes a bit, she was back.

"Here," Thrud said, thrusting a bundle

of clothes at him, along with a pair of
wool-lined boots just like hers. "Put
these on. Then I'll show you around and
take you to Goldbristle."

It was blissful to be warm again, Demon
thought, wiggling his fingers in his
sheepskin mittens. He had the magic
medicine box under one arm, and his
sack of supplies over his shoulder. Thrud
was striding ahead of him, pointing
things out. She'd already explained that
the fluffy stuff was called snow, and
the ice spears were icicles, laughing in
delight at Demon's ignorance. He'd tried
not to mind too much.

"That's Valhalla," she said as they
passed a huge hall full of lights and
loud laughter, with a golden tree

growing outside it. "Where the heroes and the Valkyrie shield-maidens have a permanent party. I'm not allowed in there, really, though I once sneaked in secretly."

She looked round at Demon. "They can get a bit rowdy and rude," she said, grinning, and then she sighed. "All I want is to be a shield-maiden, but first I have to do a brave deed to prove myself worthy."

But Demon wasn't listening properly. He had spotted an enormous stag and a gigantic nanny goat, standing on top of the hall, nibbling on the branches of a tree. From the stag's golden antlers poured a glistening stream of crystal water.

"Hello," he called up. "Who are you? I'm Demon from Olympus."

The stag turned its immense head. "I am Oakthorn," he said. "Nice to meet you, Demon-from-Olympus." Then he went back to nibbling.

The goat, however, leapt down. "I've heard about you," she said, butting Demon gently in the leg. "You're the one who cured my old friend Amaltheia, aren't you?" Demon nodded. "Well, mind you do the same for poor Goldbristle. I'm tired of living in the dark."

"I'll do my best," Demon said as he and Thrud walked on.

Thrud was looking at him in amazement. "Do you really know the language of all animals?" she asked. "I didn't understand any of that bleating you just did!"

"Yes," Demon said. "It's because of my dad, I think." And he explained about Pan being the god of the forest and wild beasts. Just then, they passed the biggest tree Demon had ever seen in his life.

"Whoa!" he said, stopping to gaze up and up and up. "That's some tree!"

"That's Yggdrasil, the Great Ash," said Thrud, stroking the smooth grey-green bark. "It holds the worlds together." Then her eyes narrowed as a flash of flaming red darted between its branches, leaping from twig to twig.

"And that," she said, with a frown, "is Ratatosk. We can all understand *him*!"

Ratatosk, Demon saw, was a huge red squirrel. All the beasts in Asgard seemed to be larger than life.

"Ooh! Ooh! A new visitor," he chattered. "I must spread the word!" And with that, he disappeared up the trunk and out of sight.

"Don't ever listen to Ratatosk's tall stories," Thrud instructed Demon. "He's a terrible tattletale and a liar, and he spreads gossip all around Asgard. Why, he even told on me once for borrowing Dad's hammer, and I was only *thinking* about it."

Demon looked at her. "That doesn't

sound so bad," he said. "Maybe he just exaggerates a bit."

Thrud looked at him, a dark glint in her eye. "Just you wait till he tells some awful fib about you, and you get threatened with scrubbing the ice off Odin's throne for it," she said.

Demon laughed. "Poseidon threatened to make me scrub salt off seaweed for a hundred years, once," he said.

"That's not as bad as the time Loki tricked me into polishing every icicle in Asgard," she said. "I only found out afterwards. He's my uncle, but you'd better watch out for him, too. Dad says he's a dangerous maniac!"

Her eyes went big and round, and

her voice lowered to a whisper.

"He caused a terrible fight between all the gods not long ago, and Odin All-Father had to lock him up in prison for a long time. He's out now, but Dad says he's threatened to take his revenge on all Asgard."

By the time they got to Goldbristle's stable, they had traded many stories about awful things the gods had threatened them with, and were on the road to being firm friends.

As soon as Demon saw the boar, his heart sank. The beast was nearly as big as a wagon, and it was lying on its side, with tears flowing out from under its long, pale piggy eyelashes and over its long, brutal-looking tusks. It gave off a sickly greenish-golden glow, and it was groaning piteously. Frey was sitting in the straw, stroking the boar's hairy ears.

"He's even worse than when we left," said Frey. "The whole of Asgard is counting on you to cure him, Pandemonius."

It was a big responsibility. Demon examined Goldbristle all over, but there was nothing obvious wrong. He tapped the magic medicine box.

"Wake up, box," he said. "We have a patient."

The box glowed blue all over, and gave a sort of quiver.

"State nature of ailment," it said in

its tinny voice.

"Goldbristle's light has gone out," Demon said. "Maybe it's a bit like the problem we had with the Cretan Bull." The Cretan Bull had lost its fire when horrible Heracles dragged it through the sea.

The box snapped open, and out whipped a series of thin bright blue tentacles with suckers all down them, which attached themselves to Goldbristle's body, including one that probed inside his mouth.

"What are THOSE?" Demon asked. The box had never produced anything like that before.

"Upgrade 2.1, copyright Hephaestus

Productions," said the box. "Now initiating test mode."

On its lid, a tiny rainbow began to whirl round and round, filling the stable with colour. Demon, Frey and Thrud waited in a breathless silence that went on, and on, and on . . .

"Hurry up, box," Demon said eventually. "We haven't got all day." With a loud *pop*, the suckers detached themselves and shot back inside.

"Running diagnostics," it said.

"What's it saying?" Thrud asked. With a start, Demon realised she couldn't understand it. He'd been speaking Asgardian without even noticing, but the box didn't have the same gift.

"Nothing important yet," he said. But as he spoke, the box spat out some blue sparks.

"Patient suffering from Porcine Skotadilitiriotitis," it said.

Demon glared at it. "Explain properly," he said.

"Also known as Piggy Darkness Poison," it said, rather snarkily. "No cure ingredients in medicine cache at this time."

"What do you mean, no cure ingredients in medicine cache?" Demon asked. His stomach felt as if a big lump of snow had just landed in it. "What does that even mean? There must be something we can do."

A blue tentacle shot out and rummaged at the bottom of Demon's bag, coming out with the tiny lidded silver cauldron in which he was keeping Hestia's fire. Before Demon could do more than open his mouth, the magic medicine box had swallowed it, and then spat out a small golden bottle that glowed a bright hot orange.

"Temporary alleviation of symptoms only," said the box. "Correct-cure ingredients may be available locally."

"What correct-cure ingredients?" Demon asked. "And where do I find them?"

But the box had shut itself down and refused to respond.

6

The White Fox

Very carefully, because the boar's
tusks were sharp, Demon tipped half
the potion down Goldbristle's throat,
thinking furiously. The box hadn't
said there wasn't a cure, just that the
right ingredients might be available
locally. That meant that there must be
something here in Asgard – he just had
to find it.

As the last drop of fiery liquid
dribbled in, Goldbristle started to glow a
little brighter, then brighter still, till the
stall was bathed in a warm, golden light.

Thrud clapped her hands. "Look, Uncle Frey! He's done it!" she crowed.

"Well done, Pandemonius," said the god as Goldbristle lumbered to its feet and grunted.

Demon turned to look up at the great boar. "How are you feeling?" he asked.

"Not so good," said Goldbristle. "My light still feels as if it's all dissolving into nothing."

"Did you eat something or drink something bad?"

The bristly head shook from side to side. "No, but my dreams are full of darkness eating the world," it said.

Demon met the round, black eyes, shiny as beetle wings and framed in long, thick lashes.

"I'll find a cure for you if it's the last thing I do," he promised.

Demon turned to Frey. "I don't think you'd better take Goldbristle out just yet, Your Golden Magnificence," he said.

Frey frowned, and it was like the sun going behind a cloud. "Why not? You've cured him, haven't you? He will keep on getting brighter, won't he?"

Demon shook his head. "It's only temporary," he said. "I don't know how long it will last. He might go out again at any minute."

Frey frowned again. "Then I must take advantage of his light while I can," he said. "Help me harness him up."

Reluctantly, Demon did as he was told. He didn't like it one bit, but he knew better than to argue with a god wearing that kind of fierce expression.

"I'm sorry," he whispered to Goldbristle as the enormous beast lumbered out of the stable, with Frey in the golden chariot behind it. But the shining boar was already rising into the sky and didn't hear him.

Immediately, the whole of Asgard began to sparkle like one big diamond. Demon had to half-close his eyes till they adjusted.

"Isn't it beautiful?" said Thrud,
clapping her hands and leaping about.
She picked up a big handful of soft
snow, shaped it into a ball and threw
it at him.

"Oof!" said Demon as it hit him right
in the face.

"Score one to Team Thrud," she
shrieked, lobbing another one at him.
Demon ducked, scooped up his own
snowball and threw it.

"Right in the hood," said Thrud,
laughing and shaking snow off her.
"Score one to Team Demon!" But just
as Demon was starting to get into the
swing of things, it all went horribly
wrong. Suddenly, the bright diamond
light began to dim, and as he looked up,

he saw Goldbristle lurch and fall from the sky.

"Oh no!" Demon said, and began to run.

With a crash, the boar bounced off the corner of a roof, leaving it in splintered ruins, and dropped into a snowdrift. Frey leapt clear of the golden chariot as it shattered on the icy ground. It was as if night had fallen all in a minute.

Demon didn't want to say *I told you so* to a god, but he felt like it, as he rubbed bruise-flower ointment into all Goldbristle's sore bits and bandaged the leg the boar had sprained in the fall. Frey was fussing around, getting in Demon's way as he worked, and he just wished Frey would go away.

"It's all my fault," the handsome god said.

Demon closed his lips around a *yes it is*, keeping it in with difficulty.

Frey put a hand on his shoulder. "You can fix him, can't you?" he asked, as Demon fed Goldbristle the other half of his medicine. This time the boar's glow was much fainter, and he was groaning piteously again.

"I hope so," Demon said. "But you can't take Goldbristle out again, you know. He was lucky he didn't get hurt much worse than he is."

"I know," said Frey, looking guilty.

He wasn't in the least bit like most of

the gods Demon knew – he wasn't scary at all.

"I think I'm missing something," Demon said. "Have you ever heard of something like a darkness poison? Because that's what my box thinks is wrong with him, and I can't find anything else that fits."

Frey sighed. "No," he said. "I haven't. But I'll ask the other Asgardians if they have. I'll go right now."

A little while later, there was a patter of feet on the roof of the stable, then two heavy thumps and the screech of claws slipping on ice. As Demon heard the thud of a falling body hitting the ground and a loud shriek, he rushed outside.

Ratatosk the squirrel was sitting on his haunches, nursing his front paw. He was chattering angrily at two giant silver-black wolves, whose eyes shone like fire. They were on their bellies, stalking towards him with their tongues hanging out.

"Squirrel snacks," growled one.

"Spy supper," howled the other.

"Hey!" said Demon, stepping between them. "Leave him alone. Can't you see he's hurt?"

The wolves slunk away, snarling, before Demon even had a chance to find out who they were.

"What have you done to yourself?"

he asked the squirrel. "Let me see."

Ratatosk held out his paw, which was dripping with blood. "Horrid creatures," he said. "Chasing poor Ratatosk like that."

"Who were those wolves, anyway?" Demon asked.

"The All-Father's nasty pets, Ravenous and Greedy. They eat all his food and don't even leave a crumb for little Ratatosk." The squirrel whimpered a little. "Poor Ratatosk, nobody likes him."

"Well, I do," said Demon, fetching a bandage and some ointment from his bag. "You seem like someone who knows everything. Maybe you can help me." As he cleaned and dressed the paw, he explained about needing to find the right ingredients to cure Goldbristle.

"But I have no idea where to start," Demon finished.

"Ratatosk will help," said the squirrel. "Ratatosk will run very fast up and down the Great Ash and ask all his friends, even the scary worm. Ratatosk can find out *anything*," he boasted.

"Don't run too fast," said Demon. "You take care of that paw, now."

But the squirrel had already gone.

Demon spent the next two days looking after Goldbristle and racking his brains for a cure. Thrud kept him company sometimes, but she wasn't a big help since she knew nothing about medicine. The magic medicine box couldn't seem to give him any more useful information.

Demon's life wasn't made any easier by Ravenous and Greedy, who had taken to following him around with their tongues hanging out, threatening to bite big chunks out of him unless he made some progress – fast. And the All-Father's two ravens, Thought and Memory, were always hovering overhead, watching him.

Altogether, it made Demon very nervous. What if he couldn't find a cure? Would Odin freeze him into an icicle statue and use him for spear practice? Or would he just let the wolves and ravens tear him apart and eat him?

Demon wasn't getting much sleep, either. That first night, Thrud had turned up at the stable again and shown him to his room, which was a tiny cubbyhole above Valhalla, lined with cosy sheepskins. Unfortunately, as Thrud had warned, it was very noisy indeed.

The warriors and the Valkyrie shield-maidens below him were constantly drinking mead and singing rude songs that made him blush. They also seemed to have a game where they threw axes into the ceiling. One had crashed through the floorboard by Demon's foot, making him huddle into a corner till it was time to get up. In the end, he'd used some wax from his medicine bag to block his ears, and hoped that the axes would keep on missing him.

The only good news was that
Demeter was somehow helping to make
things grow again. She'd set up a huge
greenhouse made of some kind of ice
panels that didn't melt, and had lit it
with the special lamps she'd borrowed
from Helios. It shone like a lone beacon
amid the darkness of Asgard.

By the third night, Demon was nearly
in despair. He'd made no progress,
and Frey wasn't being any help at
all. Apparently none of the gods and
goddesses had ever heard of a darkness
poison. Even Ratatosk hadn't been able
to find anything out. And then, with a
great clangor of bells and horns, the
alarm sounded.

"Frost Giant attack! Frost Giant attack!"
shouted a great voice, and with a clatter

of armour and swords and running feet, Asgard emptied. As Demon watched, a posse of Valkyrie shield-maidens flew past him, along with a band of warrior heroes, then Thor with his hammer at his belt and a one-handed god Demon didn't recognise. Soon all was silent.

"What am I going to do?" he groaned into his hands as he sat alone on his pile of sheepskins. Even Thrud, it seemed, had deserted him.

With a pitter-patter of delicate, black-tipped paws, a white fox trotted into the room. It had eyes as green as emeralds and fur as soft as a cloud.

"I can help," it said, sitting down in front of Demon and curling its tail around its feet.

"Who are you?" Demon asked. "Did Ratatosk send you?"

The fox cocked its head to one side, bright eyes watching him as its tongue lolled out in a foxy laugh. "You may call me Trixietoes," it said. "And let's just say a little birdie told me you needed some information."

Demon leaned forward eagerly. "I definitely do need information. Can you tell me how to cure Goldbristle?"

"I can't," said Trixietoes, "but I can take you to someone who can. Have you heard of Fafnir?"

Demon shook his head.

"Shame on you," said the fox, lightly.

"Not heard of the great ice dragon, Fafnir? The terror of the world? The collector of stories? Fafnir of the fearless soul, who guards his hoard of gold and gems with a fire so cold it burns?"

"No," said Demon, a little sourly. "I'm not from here."

"Never mind. Fafnir knows everything. He will be able to find a cure for your little piggy friend. But the way is dark and dangerous, and there will be a price to pay."

"What price?" Demon asked. This fox was not giving him a good feeling, and he wasn't sure he trusted it.

"Now, where would be the fun in

telling you that?" said Trixietoes. "Are you coming or not?"

"Coming," said Demon, scrambling into his clothes and boots. He'd been in dark and dangerous places before. And after all, how bad could a fox's price be? It would probably be like the griffin and just want some extra meat. If it got him the ingredients he needed to cure Goldbristle, it would be worth it.

As Trixietoes led him through the back ways of Asgard, through narrow alleyways and then into a dark tunnel that led steeply downwards, Demon suddenly remembered his dad's warning. *Don't go near any dark ice caves.* All at once, his stomach was full of icy prickles that flowed up over his shoulders and down his spine.

"Hey!" he called. "Trixietoes! Where, exactly, are you taking me?"

But the fox had disappeared around a corner, and as Demon spoke, rough hands seized him.

"Help!" he tried to call, fighting with everything he had against the dark-cloaked figures that surrounded him. But despite his best efforts, a large sack was jammed over his head and body, and a sweet-smelling cloth was forced inside the sack. Demon felt his head begin to spin, and his cries slurred into mumbles. He was picked up and slung over a bony shoulder, and then he knew nothing more.

7

Svartalfheim

Demon woke to find himself in pitch darkness, tied up hand and foot. His head felt as if it had been stuffed with scratchy burnt grass, and his mouth tasted like hundred-year-old, hundred-armed monster dribble. There was a strange buzzing noise right by his ear, as if a fly was hovering there. He tried to move, but as soon as he did, whatever was holding him burned his wrists and ankles with a hiss of freezing air.

"Oh, I wouldn't do that if I were you," said an amused voice close beside him.

"I'd hate for you to lose an extremity."

Demon cracked open an eye and peered into the darkness, but he couldn't see anyone or anything.

"W-who are you?" he whispered, trying not to let his voice shake with terror.

"Well, I suppose I *should* introduce myself properly," said the voice, which had now moved in front of him. Gradually a sickly green light began to glow out of the walls, revealing a tall thin figure with a pointy beard, wearing a silver helmet with a shiny green gem stuck to it. Demon recognised him at once. It was the god he'd noticed right at the back of the line of gods and goddesses when the cloud ship arrived in Olympus. The one who'd been so hard to see properly.

"But you're a god!" he gasped.

"Yes," the god agreed. "I am, indeed. The god Loki, to be precise, Master Pandemonius. But if you like, you can call me Trixietoes." In a dazzling flash of light, the white fox reappeared where the god had been, and then disappeared again to leave Loki standing there once more, a wild, wicked look of triumph on his face.

Tricksy, *indeed*, Demon thought, though he didn't say it aloud, and with a sickening lurch of his heart, he remembered what Thrud had said about her uncle Loki. *He's a dangerous maniac . . . He's threatened to take his revenge on all Asgard.*

"Why have you brought me here?"
Demon asked.

"Oh, that," said Loki, carelessly.
"Well, I couldn't have you mending old
Goldbristle, now, could I? After I've
gone to so much trouble to poison him,
I mean."

Demon was so furious that he lunged
for the god, then hissed with pain as his
shackles burned him again.

"How could you?" he yelled. The
anger seemed to have chased all
the fear out of him. "What has poor
Goldbristle ever done to you?"

"Well, nothing, really," said Loki. "But

I was annoyed with Odin and the others, so I decided to take their light away." His lips curled away from his teeth in an ugly snarl. "Nobody puts me in prison and gets away with it."

Demon thought furiously. If he could flatter Loki into telling him what poison he'd used, maybe somehow he could escape and find a cure. He squashed down his anger with an effort and forced an admiring look onto his face.

"So you didn't just trick me," Demon said, opening his eyes very wide. "You tricked all the gods, as well. Nobody has a clue how you did it, so you must be very clever. I've never had a failure with curing a beast before – but you definitely beat me. However did you do it?"

Loki laughed, evilly. "They don't call me the Father of Lies for nothing," he said. "But it wasn't easy. I had to steal a drop of darkness, right from the heart of the earth. Once a creature of light has eaten that, nothing will cure it but a drop of old Fafnir's blood, dripped onto an ice diamond, then ground up and mixed with some Fenrir wolf spit. Have fun finding those! Oh, wait . . ." he paused for effect, a sneer on his face. "You can't. Because you're going to be locked up down here FOREVER! Have fun with the dark elves, little healer!"

And with another evil laugh, Loki shimmered into a bright green fly and buzzed off through the bars of the silver gate that now appeared in the wall.

Immediately, two terrifying figures appeared outside. As they unlocked the gate and entered the dungeon, Demon cowered back, knowing that these must be the dark elves that had captured him. They wore black hoods that covered their faces, so all he could see were two pairs of white eyes with red pupils, and the bony green hands that now reached out for him, their pointed nails filthy and clotted with what looked like dark red blood.

"Leave me alone!" he cried, flinching as his shackles burned him for a third time.

"Don't be foolish, boy from Olympus," said the taller of the two, and Demon caught a flash of sharp teeth. "We're here to take off your bonds. Hold still, or it will be the worse for you!" Demon held still as the creature traced a complicated pattern over each of his bonds, which melted away into nothing.

"Here," said the other, shoving a stone plate at him that held a glowing mound of something black and slimy, together with a mug of oily water. "The best Svartalfheim cuisine! Enjoy!" It chuckled like a stream running over knives.

"I-is that where I am, then?" Demon asked, trying to keep his voice steady.

"Why, yes, young master. It is. And we are your personal jailers, Grod and Cinder." The creature who spoke bowed with a mocking flourish.

"Pleased to meet you," said Demon stoutly. Maybe he could persuade them to let him go if he was polite enough.

"Ooh!" said the one he thought was Cinder. "Listen to its lovely manners!"

The other dark elf put its face near to Demon. "Lovely manners don't open locks," Grod hissed. "So don't think you'll get around us that way."

Faster than a midnight whirlwind, they spun away from him and out through the gate, locking it behind them.

"Bye for now," they jeered. "Don't go anywhere!" And then they were gone.

Demon paced around his dungeon, trying not to panic. There was a kind of rough pallet of rags in one corner, but there were no windows, and when he touched the silver bars of the gate, they threw him backwards to the other side of the cell in a welter of scarlet sparks. He hit the glowing green wall with a thump and slid down it, landing on his bottom on the rough stone floor, trying to control his breathing, but it was no good.

"Help!" he screamed angrily. "Odin! Thor! Thrud! Someone, help me!" But all he heard as he lay there, choking back tears of rage, were echoes of his own voice, and then silence.

Eventually Demon sat up, wiping

his nose with the back of his hand. Somewhere in the scuffle back in Asgard, he had lost his sheepskin mittens, and now his hands were freezing. He tucked them under his armpits to try to warm them.

Come on, Demon, he thought. *There has to be some way to get out of this.* He looked in the pouch at his waist. His dad's pipes were no good – he knew that. Olympus was too far away for the music to reach. And there was nothing else in the pouch but a few pinches of dried herbs, an acorn, a scrap of parchment he'd made some notes on, and a stub of charcoal.

Then all at once he became aware of a pulse of warmth in the middle of his chest.

"Of course! The phoenix feather!" he gasped, suddenly remembering that he had it with him. But then he looked around his cold, dank dungeon, and his momentary joy trickled out of his toes like water.

The phoenix had told him to throw the feather into a sandalwood fire if he was ever in great danger and then help would come. Well, if ever Demon had needed help, it was now. He had the sandalwood in a little pouch around his neck, but how was he ever going to light a fire in this dark, damp place?

There were no torches in this prison, not even any light except for the green glow in the walls, and Hestia's fire had been used up by the magical medicine box. Demon didn't even have a flint with him to strike a spark.

"How could I have been so stupid?" he groaned. "I'm a total idiot." What hope did he have now of escaping this terrible place?

8

The Blood of Fafnir

Demon looked around his dungeon
one more time, just in case, but again
he saw nothing that might help. He
stumbled over to the rag pallet in
despair, and sat down. Right away,
there was a cracking sound and he
leapt up again with a yelp. He'd sat on
something sharp.

Rubbing the bruise on his bottom,
he lifted up the rags, which smelled
horribly, like something had died on
them. Underneath was a spike of shiny
black rock with the tip broken off. That

must have been what snapped. Demon looked at it. Maybe, just maybe, it was the answer to his prayers.

Scrabbling frantically with his cold fingers, he picked it up and looked at it, then scraped it experimentally against the rough grey rock of the floor. It made a satisfying scritching sound.

Hands trembling with excitement, he fumbled under his clothes for the little pouch of sandalwood shavings and the feather. Then he ripped a bit of sheep's wool off the lining of his coat and made it into a tiny ball, putting some of the sandalwood on top.

Scritch-scratch-scritch went the black stone against the grey rock. Demon could feel it getting warm.

"Come on!" he said. "Make a spark!"
But however hard he willed it to come,
no spark appeared.

Despair settled into him like a deep
fog, but just as he had admitted defeat
and was gloomily gathering up the fire
ingredients and the feather again, he
heard a tiny pattering sound and a loud
sniff. Quickly, he shoved everything
inside his coat. Someone – or something
– was here, and he wasn't going to
risk his one hope of escape being
discovered.

"Who's that?" he whispered, hoping it
wasn't Cinder and Grod again.

There was a squeak, and outside the
bars appeared the furry red figure of
Ratatosk the squirrel. Demon felt a

great wave of relief crash over him.

"Oh, thank Zeus!" he said. "I thought nobody was ever going to find me down here."

"Ratatosk was clever," said the squirrel. "Ratatosk saw you go off with the wicked Loki fox and followed."

"Well, I'm glad you did, Ratatosk," Demon said gratefully. "You are definitely the cleverest squirrel in the whole world. Now, can you get me out of here?"

The squirrel shook its head. "Ratatosk can't open elf locks. They bite."

Demon felt his excitement drain away, but then he had an idea. "Well, if you can't open the lock, could you find me a bit of fire? Maybe a torch or something?"

The squirrel cocked its head to one side. "Maybe," he said. "Ratatosk will try." And with that, he scampered off.

Demon paced around the dungeon while he waited, stamping his feet to keep warm. It was so cold now that his breath was freezing into tiny cloud crystals in front of his face. Sooner than he'd hoped, he heard the patter of paws again. Ratatosk was back, and, even better, he held in his paws a flickering torch that trailed black, foul-smelling smoke.

"Ratatosk stole the fire!" he chattered. "It nearly burned his tail!"

"Can you pass it through the bars
without touching them?" Demon asked.
He didn't want Ratatosk to be hurt.

Eventually, with great care and a few
near misses, Demon held the torch in
his hands. He crouched down, looking
into Ratatosk's inquisitive black eyes.

"Will you do one more thing for me?"
he asked. "Will you go and tell Thrud
what's happened and where I am?
Maybe if I can't get out by myself, Thor
could come and rescue me when he's
back from fighting giants."

The squirrel's ears drooped. "Thrud
doesn't like Ratatosk," he said. "She
won't believe me."

Demon thought for a minute, then

leaned the torch carefully against the wall and pulled out the scrap of parchment and the charcoal from his pouch.

"Yes, she will," he said, scrubbing out his notes and drawing a series of pictures on the smeary surface. He slipped it under the bars. "Give her this."

As the squirrel scampered off again, Demon could only hope that Thrud would be able to interpret his scrawls. He hadn't dared write anything, in case she couldn't read.

Carefully he built his tiny fire again and set light to it. Once the sandalwood was ablaze, he threw the precious gold-and-red feather in.

"Phoenix!" he cried. "Come to my aid!"

There was a great whoosh of flame that lit up the dark dungeon. The sickly green glow of the walls turned blue and began to glitter strangely, and then, with a high, sweet burst of song, the phoenix was there, and the fire disappeared, leaving behind a pleasant fragrance in the air.

"How can I help, O Protector of the Phoenix?" the bird said in its beautiful voice.

Demon explained about Loki and how Goldbristle had been poisoned.

"And now I need to get an ice diamond and find this dragon Fafnir and get a drop of his blood," he said, all in a rush. "Oh, and also some spit from a wolf called Fenrir. But before I do any of that, I have to get out of here."

The phoenix looked at him. "That's quite some task, young healer. Getting out of here won't be easy, and if I know Fafnir, he won't be too eager to give you his blood. But the ice diamond I can help with. There are plenty here."

"Where?" Demon asked, but the bird was already pecking at one of the strange glitters in the walls.

Just as the phoenix dropped a sparkly white pebble at his feet, Demon became aware of harsh shouts outside and the sound of running feet.

"Oh no!" he said, picking up the

pebble, which felt like a drop of pure frost in his hand, and putting it in his pouch. "The dark elves are coming!"

"Then hold onto my tail, Pandemonius, and don't let go, whatever you do!"

Demon grabbed the phoenix's long, fiery tail and hoped he that he wouldn't get burnt. But though the flames licked and curled around his hands and arms, it just felt pleasantly warm.

"How do we . . ." he started, but the bird was already flying straight up, towards the ceiling. "Wha—"

His voice cut off as the phoenix flew *into* the stone, pulling Demon behind it. It was the oddest sensation of Demon's life, even stranger than being towed

through space and time by Golden Dog.
He could feel himself flowing through
the stone as if it were water. After
what seemed like a very long time,
there was a *pop*, and they exited the
spire of a tall ice mountain.

"I'll take you to Fafnir," called the
phoenix. "You'll need me to protect you
from the poison around his lair."

Demon was too busy clinging on and
checking if all his body parts were still
there to answer.

A full moon shone overhead, lighting
up the brilliant white ice below, and
the stars blazed across the sky like a
string of crystal jewels. Demon was just
thinking how beautiful it was when the

ice suddenly became grey and cracked, with smoke rising from it. Pools of stagnant water lay here and there, with what looked like sticky black fungus at their edges, and occasionally they made loud slurping blop noises.

The grey stretched as far as his eye could see, eventually rising up into a gigantic black mountain wreathed in plumes of noxious steam. Demon had a nasty feeling he knew where they were headed.

As they descended towards a jagged cave entrance, the phoenix began to glow, emitting a pale rose-coloured mist that twined around Demon, who had begun to cough and splutter as the fumes hit his lungs. Immediately he felt better.

"Stay within my mist," the phoenix called as they landed. "It will protect you. And let me do the talking."

The first thing Demon noticed was the terrible smell. The second thing he noticed was the glittering heap of gold and gems, which slid and crunched beneath his feet like autumn leaves on a frozen pond.

Unfortunately, the third thing he noticed was the pair of eyes high above him. The eyes were huge and round as millstones, and red with a golden slit right in the middle.

"Who dares to disturb Fafnir?" came a great grumble of a voice.

"I am the phoenix of the Mountains of

Burning Sand," it said. "And I bring my companion, Pandemonius of Olympus, to ask a boon!"

"A boon?" Fafnir bellowed. "You lie! You are robbers and thieves, come to steal my hoard!" A gout of pure white flame roared out of its mouth, surrounding both the phoenix and Demon. Demon ducked, but the fire just bounced off the pink mist, to his great relief.

"We already have the only jewel we need," said the phoenix. "But with your help, this young man can save all of Asgard from darkness."

"Is that so?" asked Fafnir, sounding intrigued, and Demon remembered that Trixietoes had called the dragon a collector of stories. "How?"

"My companion will explain."

So Demon cleared his throat and told the story of Goldbristle and Loki once more. As soon as he got to the part about Loki, Fafnir roared again, so that the very rocks around them shook.

"That thief, that renegade, that black-hearted weasel-tosser of a god! So he's responsible for the darkness, is he? How dare he?"

More white flames shot out, towards the ceiling this time, which sprouted smoking icicles as big as stalactites, and then the dragon lowered its pale spiked head, stretching out its neck towards Demon. He tried not to breathe, or to look at the shreds of rotten meat caught in the beast's arm-length teeth.

"Very well," said the dragon. "What do you need from me, youngling?"

"Just one drop of your blood on this ice diamond, O wise and mighty Fafnir," said Demon, pulling the sparkly pebble from his pouch and holding it out.

Delicately for such a huge creature, Fafnir lifted one gigantic foreleg, extended a long, curved talon and pierced its other leg. A stream of steaming blood ran out, hissing as it hit the gold beneath. Demon willed his hand not to tremble as the talon hovered over his fingers, one drop of scarlet gore hanging from its tip. It fell, hitting the ice diamond square in the middle, sinking in immediately and turning the jewel red as fire. Quickly, Demon stowed it in his pouch again.

"Thank you, great one," he said, bowing low. "Now all I have to get is some spit from Fenrir, and Goldbristle will be cured."

Fafnir let out a bellow of dragonish laughter.

"Drool from the mad wolf?" he roared. "I wish you luck with that, my young friend. Be careful you do not suffer the same fate as poor Tyr One-Hand. Now, go. I feel a hunger coming upon me. I wouldn't want to mistake you for dinner."

Demon didn't wait to be told. He

grabbed the phoenix's tail again, and soon they were soaring through the air towards Asgard.

"I will have to leave you now," the phoenix called, swooping down to land outside Goldbristle's stable. "I must return to my mountains and sing the fire devils their nightly lullaby."

"Thank you for saving me," Demon said. But his only answer was a second phoenix feather swirling down to land at his feet. He picked it up and stowed it carefully against his chest, where once again it made a small, comforting warmth against his heart.

9

The Mad Wolf

Almost as soon as he had landed, Thrud came skidding round the corner.

"Where have you been?" she yelled. "Ratatosk just told me some parcel of lies about you being kept prisoner down in Svartalfheim. And what does *this* mean?" She waved the bit of parchment at him.

"Ratatosk wasn't telling a pack of lies," Demon said, suddenly angry. "You should give him some credit. And that," he said, grabbing the piece of parchment, "was me trying to get you to ask your dad to come and rescue me. But don't worry. I got out, anyway, no thanks to you."

He turned to go into Goldbristle's stable, seething.

The boar was lying on its side, its light almost gone, and Demon's anger evaporated as quickly as it had come. He ran over to the enormous creature and reached up to stroke its bristly head.

"Don't worry, Goldbristle," he said. "I've nearly got a cure. I just have to get some Fenrir spit, and you'll be right as rain in no time."

He heard a tiny cough behind him and

turned to see Thrud standing there, looking a bit sheepish.

"I'm sorry I yelled at you," she said. "But I was just so worried when you disappeared. I've been all alone since everyone went off to fight the giants. And I'm sorry I didn't believe Ratatosk. Were you really captured by Loki and the dark elves? How on earth did you get out?"

Demon told Thrud the whole story. By the end, her mouth had turned into a big round O, and if her eyes had got any bigger, they would have popped out of her head.

"You went to see *Fafnir*?" she gasped. "How are you even still alive?"

"Well, it was all because of the phoenix, really," Demon said modestly. He looked at her and sighed. "But now I have to find Fenrir the wolf. Do you know where he is?"

Thrud nodded slowly. "I do," she said. "Ever since he bit off Uncle Tyr's hand, he's been chained up on an island in the middle of our lake. Dad says he's quite mad and I'm forbidden to go anywhere near him. But I know how to get there." She looked as if she was thinking, hard.

Even though there was nobody around, she lowered her voice. "You know I was telling you about having to do a brave deed to prove myself worthy of being a shield-maiden? Well, I'm thinking that if I row you out to

Fenrir's island, that would count as one, wouldn't it?"

"I should think so," said Demon. "Though I wonder if he really is mad. Perhaps it's just that he's been tied up and alone for so long."

Thrud gave him a long look. "Trust me," she said. "He's mad. Odin loves wolves, and he only tied Fenrir up because some old prophecy says Fenrir's meant to kill him. Now, come on, hurry up." She cocked an ear, listening. "Everyone will be coming back from fighting the giants soon. We need to steal a boat *right now*. With any luck they'll all be either feasting or asleep by the time we get back."

Thrud, it turned out, was almost as good at sneaking around Asgard as the white fox had been. The difference was, though, that this time Demon knew he wasn't going to be kidnapped.

Soon they were creeping onto a long pier, jutting out into a lake so big that Demon couldn't even guess where the far shore was under the darkness. A series of long, low boats with high prows were tied up alongside.

"Come on," said Thrud, climbing into a boat made of some kind of pale wood and shaped like a swan. "Let's take this one. It belongs to Idunn. She'll never notice. That goddess of yours – Demeter – has got her working in that big greenhouse, trying to make her apple trees come into fruit."

Demon rather hoped Demeter
wouldn't notice them, either. He didn't
want her reporting back any trouble to
Zeus – though she hadn't exactly taken
any notice of anything he'd done so far.
But since getting the spit from Fenrir
was a key part of getting Goldbristle
better, he thought he'd probably be
forgiven.

"Get comfortable and keep quiet,"
Thrud ordered him. "We don't want
the lake serpents to hear us." She
pushed off and started to row, with
long, steady strokes that hardly broke
the surface of the still water. Demon
lay there, looking up at the stars and
wondering why they were so different
from the ones that shone above

Olympus. Then he let out a small gasp. On the far horizon, waves of colour were dancing – billowing curtains of pale green and pink and blue moving across the sky. Thrud saw him looking.

"The Nimble Dancers," she whispered very quietly. "Some say they've been up there since before the All-Father himself." Then, all at once, she let out a muffled scream and shook her oars, making the boat rock dangerously. Demon saw a ripple in the water and a dozen slimy heads broke the surface on each side. They twined about the oar blades, biting and snapping with their sharp needle teeth.

"Lake serpents," Thrud said, her voice slightly desperate. "They never give up till they've eaten their prey. I'll try and

fight them off." She pulled out a small
dagger from her belt and bent towards
the beasts on the left-hand side.

But Demon had already pulled out
his dad's pipes. He put them to his lips
and started to play. Immediately, all
the serpents went limp and slid off the
oars, slipping back into the water and
disappearing below, to Thrud's evident
surprise and relief.

"Phew!" he said. "I wasn't sure these
were going to work up here."

After what seemed like hours had
passed, the island loomed up before
them. Thrud beached the boat on a
small point of frozen sand.

"This way," she said, unsheathing her dagger again. "And whatever you do, don't get anywhere near his jaws."

"No stabbing," said Demon sternly. He wasn't allowing any beast to be hurt on his watch. "I'll use my pipes again if I have to, but I have to get near enough to collect some of his drool, or there's no point in us being here."

Thrud rolled her eyes. "I said I would do a brave deed, not a stupid one. I promise I won't stab him unless I have to, though," she said, and Demon had to be content with that.

The path wound up and up through the rocky cliffs and Demon was out of breath by the time they reached the top. When he got there, he saw a gigantic round boulder set into the earth, with what looked like a ghostly greeny-gold silk ribbon wound round and round it, and anchored to a tall stone post which had been driven right through the middle of it. Attached to the ribbon was the biggest wolf he'd ever seen, fast asleep and curled around the boulder as if it were a tiny pebble.

"How on Olympus does that little ribbon hold such a big creature?" he whispered, no more than a breath of sound in Thrud's ear.

"It's stronger than it looks," she whispered back. "Fenrir broke three huge chains before they tried this one. Dad says the dwarves made it of six things: the sound of a cat's paws, a giantess's beard, the roots of a mountain, the sinews of a bear, the breath of a fish, and bird spit."

Demon wasn't sure most of those things even existed, but as he himself had had to capture a maiden's sigh and the high and low notes from a lyre to cure Hades' pet three-headed dog, Cerberus, he wasn't going to argue. He didn't like the fact that Fenrir was tied up at all, though, and when they got closer, he started to get really angry. He seized Thrud by the arm.

"What did they do that for?" he whispered, pointing. The poor beast's jaws were pinned open with a long, golden sword, so that his tongue rolled out onto the ground. Demon could see that there would be no trouble collecting drool – streams of it were running out of Fenrir's mouth and dribbling into the ground with a sound like a trickling drain.

"To stop him biting, I suppose," Thrud whispered back. "But it doesn't look very nice, does it?"

"It does *not*. And I'm going to get it out."

Before Thrud could do more than hiss a frantic *no* at him, Demon strode forward, ready to help the poor creature or die trying. But as he did so, his foot landed on a pile of dry heather and sank into it with a sharp *crack*.

Fenrir was awake immediately, leaping up with a long, wavering *arroooo*, and lunging at them, his eyes fiery red and his jaws flinging drool and foam about in bloody red strings. Although Demon could understand every beast alive, he couldn't make head or tail of what Fenrir was saying. It just sounded like mad gibberish, apart from two words.

"Kill Odin," Fenrir was howling over and over. "Kill Odin."

Then he started to choke as the green-gold ribbon seemed to tighten about his throat, and the words and gibberish cut off into a kind of strangled gargle.

"Quick!" shouted Thrud. "Play your pipes."

Demon already had them in his hand,

and jamming them against his lips, he
played his dad's special emergency
twiddle.

Nothing happened at first, and then,
very, very slowly, the great wolf
collapsed, as if all the strings in his
joints had been cut. His eyes closed and
he lay utterly still.

"Oh, poor thing," Demon said,
his voice all choked up. "Poor, poor
Fenrir." Slowly, he walked over to the
huge sleeping body and tried to pry
the gaping jaws further open so that
he could get the sword free. But he
couldn't do it by himself.

"Help me," he begged Thrud, and with
her very nervous assistance, Demon
eased the sword out and threw it as

far away as he could. It hit the frozen ground with a mournful clang that echoed the one in Demon's heart. The moment he'd laid hands on the wolf, he'd felt the wrongness inside the beast, like veins of poisonous red and black hate invisible to the eye. For the first time in his life, Demon knew there was nothing he could do to cure this creature. Fenrir was truly, completely lost to madness.

With tears rolling down his cheeks, Demon cleansed Fenrir's wounds as best he could, then pulled up clumps of dry, dead grass and tucked them around the great wolf's body, making a kind of cosy nest for him. Thrud was crying, too, sitting on the boulder beside the sleeping beast and stroking his ragged black ears.

Finally, Demon was done. He pulled out the corked jar he'd brought from his pouch and scooped up some of the red-tinged drool.

"Sleep is the only thing I can give him," he said as he and Thrud walked back down the cliff path. "I don't know how long the spell will last, but it might be forever, if I don't play the notes to wake him up."

"Then may he sleep till Ragnarok and the end of the world," she said, sniffing. "And may his dreams be full of light."

10

The Stolen Hammer

When Demon and Thrud got back to
Asgard, it was ablaze with candles and
the sound of celebration. But Demon
didn't feel like celebrating. Even though
he now had the last ingredient he
needed to make Goldbristle's medicine,
Demon still felt miserable at leaving
Fenrir. Maybe if he'd been able to call
Morpheus, the spirit of dreams, he
might have been able to help, as he had
with the man-eating mares, but Demon
somehow doubted it. Fenrir was no
ordinary beast. He was the brother of
Jormungand, the scary worm who coiled

around the roots of the world, and of Hel, goddess of the dead, Thrud had told him after their long, silent journey back across the lake.

"So he's not just an immortal – he's half a god," she finished, as they were walking back to Goldbristle's stable, avoiding staggering knots of warriors on their way to feast in Valhalla. Demon gave a deep sigh.

"Well, at least I get to cure Goldbristle now," he said. As soon as they were inside, he got out his pestle and mortar, dropped in the ice diamond and started to pound it.

"Better . . . turn . . . it . . . into . . . dust . . . before . . . I . . . add . . . the . . . Fenrir . . .

spit," he panted as he brought the pestle down over and over again. Nothing happened. The ice diamond didn't even have the tiniest crack in it.

"Here, let me have a go," said Thrud. But she couldn't turn it into dust, either, or even make the tiniest dent.

"I know," said Demon. "We'll get my magic medicine box to do it."

He tapped it sharply on the lid. "Wake up, box! I've found the ingredients we need," he said.

With a blue flicker and a buzzing noise, the box came to life. "Insert item," it said in its tinny voice, and a round, mouth-like hole opened in its lid. Demon plucked the ice diamond out of

the mortar and poked it into the hole.
After a few clonks and a loud, screechy
whir, the ice diamond came flying back
out again, nearly hitting him in the eye.

"Pulverisation program damage alert,"
it said. "Initiating repairs in lockdown
mode." Immediately the rainbow wheel
began to spin on all four sides and the
hole snapped shut.

Demon felt like screaming. "Now what
are we going to do?" he said. "If we
can't crush the diamond, we can't make
the medicine."

Goldbristle groaned. "I'm going to die,
then," the boar grunted piteously.

"No, you aren't," Demon said, his
voice fierce. "I'll find a way. There must

be something strong enough to smash this thing."

Thrud was looking thoughtful.

"There might be," she said. "But it'll only work if my dad is distracted. Come with me."

Once again, they sneaked through the dark streets of Asgard, but nobody was about. Valhalla was full to bursting as they passed.

"That's good," Thrud said. "Hopefully my dad will be in there, celebrating hard. It sounds like they beat the Frost Giants again."

"What's the plan?" Demon asked.

"You'll see," she said, opening a small door at the back of the hall. The noise hit them like a thump in the chest.

"Stay here and keep guard," she said. "And if you see Greedy and Ravenous, play your pipes at them. If they catch me, they'll ruin everything."

Thrud dropped to her knees and, keeping to the shadows, crawled up to the big dais where all the deities were yelling out toasts to the brave. Demon bit back a squeak as he saw Thrud draw her dagger and cut Thor's hammer, Mjölnir, off his belt, lowering it silently to the ground. Her arms strained and her face turned beet red at the effort. Then she bent and whispered some words over it and right away she picked it up as if it were as light as air. She

scurried back to where Demon was
waiting.

"No sign of the wolves," he said.

"Good. Now let's hurry. Dad will miss
this before long, and I'll be in terrible
trouble if I don't put it back." She
looked at him sideways. "I'm not really
supposed to be able to lift it, but I
haven't been around Dad all this time
without learning a thing or two!"

Thrud said Mjölnir would break the
mortar, so Demon cleared a patch on
a clean bit of the stable floor and put
the ice diamond on it.

"One! Two! Three! Go!" said Thrud,
lifting the huge hammer above her

head. And then she dropped it. BANG!
Right on top of the jewel. With a little
sigh, the ice diamond dissolved into
sparkly red dust.

"There!" said Thrud, delighted with
herself. "I knew Mjölnir would do it.
Get to work, Demon! I need to take
this hammer back to Dad."

Moving faster than the griffin after
a meaty bone, Demon scraped the dust
into the mortar and added the contents
of the spit bottle. As he mixed the
ingredients together, they began to
glow with an incandescent yellow light.
Quickly, he picked it up.

"Open wide," he said to Goldbristle,
and tipped the whole lot into the boar's
gaping mouth.

The effect was immediate. Demon flung his arm over his eyes to keep from being blinded by the brightness as Goldbristle leapt up and did a little capering dance around the stable. Then the enormous boar burst through the doors, ran outside and galloped up into the sky, grunting with joy.

Suddenly, light shone over Asgard, and if Demon had thought it was beautiful before, now every snow crystal and icicle spear gleamed with a multitude of rainbows, making the whole place sparkle like not just one, but a million huge diamonds.

Cheers erupted within Valhalla, and all the gods, goddesses, shield-maidens and warriors poured out into the streets. With a flash, Demon saw

Demeter's big greenhouse melt into
nothing, revealing rows and rows of
plants, flowers and trees, in a riot of
green and colour, curling up before his
eyes towards Goldbristle's light.

Frey reached Demon first and threw
him into the air, before grabbing him and
giving him a god-hug that smelled of
ripe apples and the sharpness of snow.

"Three cheers for Pandemonius!"
he shouted, and the cry was taken
up by everyone there. Then, amid the
rejoicing, Odin appeared, with Greedy
and Ravenous slinking at his heels and
his ravens, as usual, perched on his
shoulders.

Demon fell to his knees, but Odin
raised him up at once.

"Well, young healer," the ruler of Asgard boomed. "My ravens say you have a tale to tell us. Come! Let us eat and drink while we hear it, young hero." He made Demon stand on the dais before them all, and between munches of a delicious kind of pastry with apples, raisins, cinnamon and sparkly white sugar, Demon told them all that had happened.

"But I couldn't have done any of it without Thrud and Ratatosk," he finished, turning to Odin. "They're the real heroes, and . . ." He took a deep breath. "And Thrud really deserves to be a shield-maiden, because she's very brave, and . . . and she fought off the lake serpents and everything."

Odin looked at him out of his one eye.

"It appears so," he said. "But before anything else, Loki must be found and dealt with. This is all his fault."

He beckoned to Thor. "Find your brother and put him in Asgard's deepest dungeon," he growled. "And this time he shall not ever come out!"

Thor nodded, fingering Mjölnir, now safely restored to his belt. "It will be my pleasure, All-Father," he said, curling one corner of his mouth in a grim smile.

Demon sat blushing through one toast, then another, and another. The gods and goddesses of Asgard certainly knew how to party – and even Demeter was joining in with the praise. Then, just as Thor slipped back into his seat with a nod at Odin, the one-eyed god thumped the table for silence.

"A great deed has been done today," he boomed, "one that songs will be sung about forever in this hall. Stand forth, Ratatosk the squirrel, Thrud Thorsdaughter, and Pandemonius, Stablemaster of Olympus."

"Ooh!" said Ratatosk, leaping down from the rafters to land in front of Odin. "Has Ratatosk been clever? Does he get a prize?"

Everyone laughed.

"He does, indeed," said Odin, producing a gigantic brown nut out of nowhere. "May you never be hungry again, for this nut cannot be lost, and will always renew itself." With a squeak of delight, Ratatosk seized the nut and bounced off Ravenous and Greedy's heads, before leaping up into the rafters. The wolves snarled after him.

"Can't catch me, sillies," the squirrel chittered, before disappearing out of the window.

"Thrud Thorsdaughter," said Odin. "You have shown bravery and initiative of the highest order. I hereby grant you the status of shield-maiden of Asgard, and give you this." He handed her a hammer, similar to Thor's but about half the size. "Meet Mjölnirina."

Thrud blushed scarlet as she mumbled her thanks and went off to sit with the other shield-maidens.

"Now, Pandemonius, son of Pan. How are we to reward you?"

Demon looked at him. "I don't need anything, really, Your Serene Snowiness," he said. "I'm just glad Goldbristle is better."

"But you shall have it, anyway," Odin said. Out of the air, he drew a beautiful medallion with an ash tree embossed on it in diamonds, and a small horn banded with gold and studded with jewels in all the seven colours of the rainbow. "I hereby award you the Order of Yggdrasil and the freedom of Asgard. You are welcome here, always. I also give you this horn, which is called Far Caller. If you are ever in direst need, Pandemonius, blow it, and the warriors of Asgard will come to your aid."

Demon gulped. It was a magnificent gift. "Th-thank you, Your Incredible Iciness," he said, bowing low, just as two black-and-silver heads peered round Odin's cloak.

"Can't we bite you just a little bit now?" Ravenous growled.

"You do look very tasty," whined Greedy.

Demon laughed. "Maybe next time, boys," he said, throwing them both a pastry.

What's the next adventure waiting for Demon back on Olympus?

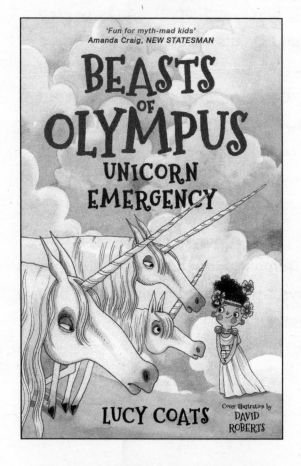

Out now, in all places good books are sold.